Mouse's Birthday Party

By Annie Cobb • Illustrated by Kathy Wilburn

Silver Press

Produced by Chardiet Unlimited, Inc. and Daniel Weiss Associates, Inc.
33 West 17th Street, New York, NY 10011

Copyright © 1991 Daniel Weiss Associates, Inc./
Chardiet Unlimited, Inc.

Illustration copyright by Kathy Wilburn

Educational Consultant:
Dr. Priscilla Lynch

GOING PLACES™ is a trademark of Daniel Weiss Associates, Inc.
and Chardiet Unlimited, Inc.

Published by Silver Press, a division of
Silver Burdett Press, Inc., Simon & Schuster, Inc.
Prentice Hall Bldg., Englewood Cliffs, NJ 07632
For information address: Silver Press.

Printed in the United States of America
10 9 8 7 6 5 4 3 2 1

Library of Congress Cataloging-in-Publication Data

Cobb, Annie
Mouse's Birthday Party/written by Annie Cobb;
illustrated by Kathy Wilburn
p.   cm.—(Going places)
Summary: On the way to Mouse's birthday party, Squirrel and
Raccoon get lost until they learn to match map symbols with
landmarks and to read street grids.
1.Going—Juvenile literature. [1.Going] I. Wilburn, Kathy, ill. II.
Title. III. Series: Going places
(Englewood Cliffs, N.J.)

ISBN 0-671-70392-7 (LSB)

ISBN 0-671-70396-X

"**O**h, dear!" said Mouse as she mailed the
invitations to her birthday party. "I hope
my friends can find my house."

Mouse had moved from the woods into town.
Her friends still lived in the woods.

"I know!" she said. "I'll send Squirrel
a map with his invitation."

Postmaster Crow gave Mouse some paper and crayons.
This is the map that Mouse made.

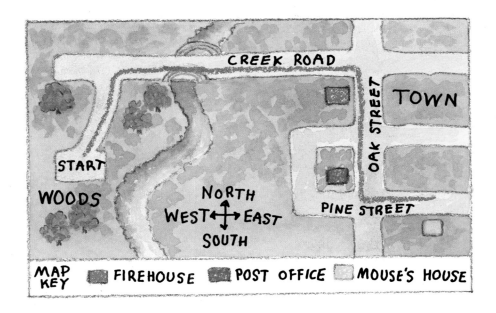

She drew streets and a red line to show the way. Then she drew little boxes to stand for some of the buildings.

At the bottom of the map, she drew the boxes again and named them.

CREEK ROAD

ODS

CREEK ROAD

TOWN

OAK STREET

PINE STREET

AIR MAIL

That afternoon, Postmaster Crow flew off
to deliver the invitations by air mail.

On the day of Mouse's birthday party, Grampy
picked up everybody in his little blue car.

Raccoon was the last to get in.

"We're late," said Raccoon. "The party starts
at two o'clock and it's two o'clock now."

"Well, Owl forgot his pillow and we had to
go back," explained Grampy. "And Bear forgot
his new hat and we had to go back.
And Squirrel forgot his map and we had to go back."

8

"Uh-oh," said Raccoon. "I forgot Mouse's birthday present."

So they had to go back again.

At last they were on their way.
By and by they came to a wooden sign
that said:

CREEK ROAD

"Which way do we go to get to
Mouse's house?" asked Grampy,
"east or west?"

"West!" shouted Raccoon.
"East!" shouted Bear.
"Quiet!" said Owl. "I'm trying to sleep."

"Wait a minute," said Squirrel.
"Mouse sent me a map."

Squirrel found Creek Road on the map.
This is what he saw.

This is what he SAW.

"Go east on Creek Road," announced
Squirrel.
"Which way shall I turn? Left?"
asked Grampy.

"Right!" answered Squirrel.
He meant *turn right*.
But Grampy thought he meant
turning *left* was the *right* thing to do.
So Grampy turned west on Creek Road,
instead of east.

This is what they DID.

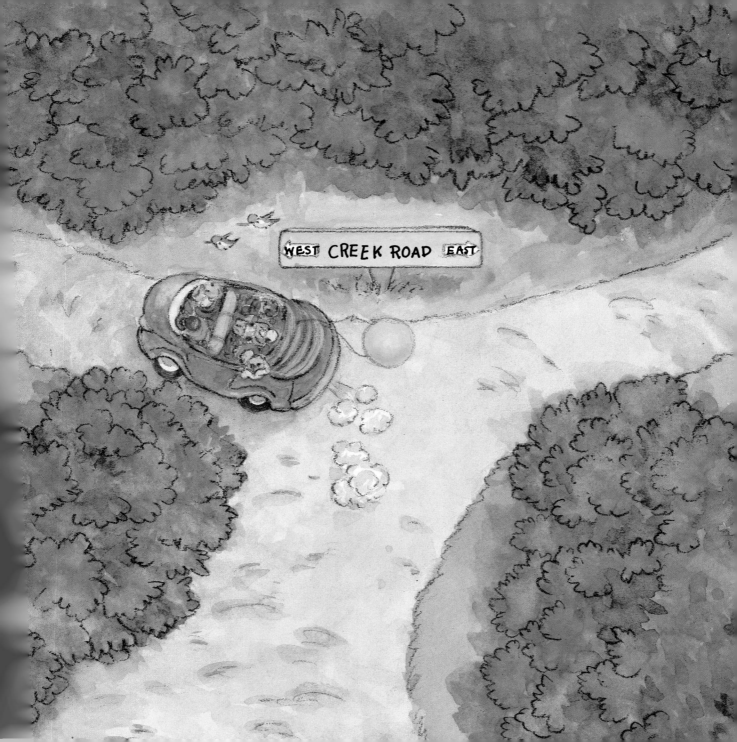

Down Creek Road went the little blue car.

Everybody began to sing "Happy Birthday,
Dear Mousie" and "Are You Sleeping, Brother
Owl?" Raccoon was just about to teach
them another song when the car
came to the end of the road. A sign said:

DEAD END

"We went the wrong way," grumbled Raccoon.

Grampy turned the car around and they
headed back the other way. They passed
the wooden sign where Grampy had made the
wrong turn. They went over a bridge.
By and by they saw another sign. It said:

YOU ARE ENTERING TOWN

"It won't be long now," said Bear.

YOU ARE
ENTERING
TOWN

This is what he SAW.

NORTH
WEST←↕→EAST
SOUTH

This is what they DID.

Squirrel looked at the map.
This is what he saw.

"When you come to the red box,
turn south on Oak Street,"
said Squirrel.

As they drove along,
everybody watched for a red box.

"Look! There's the firehouse,"
said Bear.

They kept going along Creek Road
but nobody saw a red box.

Finally they saw a sign. It said:

YOU ARE LEAVING TOWN

The little blue car bumped to a stop.

Everybody leaned over Squirrel to
look at the map.

"Hey, there's another red box at the
bottom of the map," said Bear.

Squirrel yelled, "The red box stands
for the firehouse!"

FIREHOUSE   POST OFFICE   MOUSE'S HOUSE

Grampy turned the car around and they
drove back to the firehouse.
Grampy pulled over and stopped.

"Do you know the way to Mouse's house?"
he asked Fire Chief Dog.
"We're late for Mouse's birthday party."

"Yes," said Fire Chief Dog. "Mouse
lives on Pine Street."

Grampy thanked him and drove off.
"Wait!" called Fire Chief Dog.
"I'll come too." And he jumped
into his fire engine.

"Go down Pine Street when you come to a green box.
Oh, I mean the post office," said Squirrel.

"Look!" said Bear. "There's a *real* green box
in front of the post office.
It's a mail box. And there's Pine Street."

"Hooray!" Everybody yelled.

"What is the number of Mouse's house?"
Grampy asked.

"Uh-oh," said Squirrel. "She didn't say."

Grampy pulled over and asked Postmaster Crow,
"Do you know the way to Mouse's house?
We're late for her birthday party."

This is the way
to Mouse's house.

"Yes," said Postmaster Crow. "Mouse lives
at Number 4 Pine Street. You're going
the wrong way."

24

"Wait!" called Postmaster Crow. "I have some mail for her. I'll come with you."

Grampy thanked him and drove off. Fire Chief Dog drove off, too.

They went along Pine Street.
Everybody tried to guess which house
was Mouse's.

"Mouse likes blue," said Raccoon.
"Maybe the blue house is Mouse's."
But the blue house was Number 8.
Badger lived there.

"Mouse likes tulips," said Squirrel.
"Maybe the house with tulips in the
garden is Mouse's."

But that house was Number 6.
Chipmunk lived there.

"Maybe the house with the mouse on
the porch is Mouse's," said Bear.

"MOUSE!" they shouted, when they saw
that the mouse was *their* Mouse.
"We're here!"

Everybody tumbled out of Grampy's car.

"I'm so happy to see you!" said Mouse.
"Did you have any trouble finding
my house?"

"Of course not!" said Owl, who was just
waking up. "We followed your map."

What a party!
First, they all piled into the fire engine
and went for a ride with Fire Chief Dog.

Afterwards, they went back to Mouse's
house and sang "Happy Birthday, Dear Mousie"
and had cake and ice cream.
Then Mouse opened her presents and
read all the cards brought by
Postmaster Crow.

"This is the best birthday ever,"
said Mouse.

And her friends and neighbors all agreed.